Bunny and Bee's
Forest Friends

Sam Williams

ORCHARD BOOKS

For Monty, Blackberry,
Holly, Pudding, Mango
and Paw-Paw

Also available:
Bunny and Bee's Noisy Night
Bunny and Bee's Playful Day

ORCHARD BOOKS
96 Leonard Street, London EC2A 4XD
Orchard Books Australia
32/45-51 Huntley Street, Alexandria, NSW 2015
ISBN 1 84362 184 3 (hardback)
ISBN 1 84362 599 7 (paperback)
First published in Great Britain in 2004
First paperback publication in 2005
Text and illustrations © Sam Williams 2004
The right of Sam Williams to be identified as the author
and illustrator of this work has been asserted by him in accordance
with the Copyright, Designs and Patents Act, 1988.
A CIP catalogue record for this book is available from the British Library.
(hardback) 10 9 8 7 6 5 4 3 2 1
(paperback) 10 9 8 7 6 5 4 3 2 1
Printed in Singapore

Here is a house.
A house in a tree.

The house is the home
of Bunny and Bee.

Bunny   Bee

On the roof of the house
of Bunny and Bee,

two baby squirrels
play noisily.

Chitter, chatter,

pitter, patter,

natter, clatter!

All through the forest,
spring fills the air.
Baby animals are everywhere!

"Hello," says Bunny.
"Hello," says Bee,
to the fox cubs tumbling
at the foot of the tree.

"Hello, little rabbit,"
say Bunny and Bee.

"How funny," says Bunny,
"he has long ears like me!"

A family of birds
in their nest up a tree
sing "tweet, tweet, tweet"
to Bunny and Bee.

Bunny and Bee
peer over a hedge,

to watch a fawn drink
at the water's edge.

A row of little ducklings,
one, two, three.

"Quack, quack," says Bunny.
"Quack, quack," says Bee.

Splish splash! The froglets play,
leaping and swimming
in the pond all day.

Then the forest friends

follow Bunny and Bee...

...all the way home
to their house in the tree!